CARTOON NETWORK®

by E. S. Mooney
Based on
"THE POWERPUFF GIRLS,"
as created by Craig McCracken

SCHOLASTIC INC.

New York   Toronto   London   Auckland   Sydney
Mexico City   New Delhi   Hong Kong   Buenos Aires

No part of this publication may be reproduced in whole or in part, or stored in a retrieval system, or transmitted in any form or by any means, electronic, mechanical, photocopying, recording, or otherwise, without written permission of the publisher. For information regarding permission, write to Scholastic Inc., Attention: Permissions Department, 555 Broadway, New York, NY 10012.

ISBN 0-439-25058-7

Designed by Peter Koblish

Illustrated by Mark Marderosian

12 11 10 9 8 7 6 5 4   1 2 3 4 5 6/0

Printed in the U.S.A.
First Scholastic printing, June 2001

SUGAR . . .

SPICE . . .

AND EVERYTHING NICE . . .

These were the ingredients chosen to

create the perfect little girl.

But Professor Utonium accidentally

added an extra ingredient to

the concoction —

CHEMICAL X!

And thus, The Powerpuff Girls were born!

Using their ultra superpowers,

BLOSSOM,

BUBBLES,

and BUTTERCUP

have dedicated their lives to fighting crime

and the forces of evil!

Chapter 1

The city of Townsville! And it's another happy day at Pokey Oaks Kindergarten, home of higher learning for hordes of happy Townsville tots — including, of course, our very own Powerpuff Girls.

Ms. Keane, the teacher, stood in front of the classroom taking attendance. "Bean, Julie?" she called.

Julie Bean raised her hand. "Here!"

Bubbles waited as Ms. Keane continued

reading the children's names.
She looked out the window and
noticed a pretty pink butterfly
flitting by. The butterfly's
pink wings were so pretty next to
the pretty blue sky. And the clouds looked
like cotton candy, or baby lambs, or —

Suddenly, Bubbles felt a jab in her side.
Her sister Buttercup was scowling at her.

"Stop gawking out the window," Buttercup muttered. "Your mouth was hanging
open, ya dumb bunny."

"Remember, pay attention to Ms. Keane,

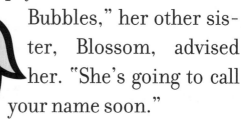

Bubbles," her other sis-
ter, Blossom, advised
her. "She's going to call
your name soon."

Bubbles looked at Blossom
with admiration. How did

Blossom always know when everyone's names were going to be called? She was so smart!

And Buttercup was so tough! Bubbles really relied on her two sisters to help her out and tell her what to do.

"Blossom?"

"Here!" Blossom answered.

"Bubbles?"

"H —" Bubbles began. But at that moment the door to the classroom burst open.

"I'm HERE!!!" yelled a loud voice.

"Oh, Princess, hello," Ms. Keane said. "You're tardy again, you know. Remember, Princess, the one thing you can't recycle is wasted time!"

"Recycle, yuck!" Princess declared. "I NEVER recycle anything. Why bother,

when my daddy can just buy me EVERY-
THING I want brand-new?"

"That's breaking Townsville Recycling
Code 304-B," Blossom told her sisters
indignantly. "She should have her
Townsville citizenship taken away!"

Bubbles didn't answer. She was too busy
staring at Princess's dress. It was the most
amazingly beautiful pink, sparkly, sequined, ribboned, ruffly dress Bubbles
had ever seen. It looked like a bridal
gown mixed with a fairy cos-
tume mixed with
a tutu.

"What a beautiful
dress," Bubbles gasped.

Princess smiled
with satisfaction.
"I know," she

said. "My daddy bought it for me. Did you notice the REAL gold trim encrusted with diamonds? LOOK."

Bubbles stared at the sparkling gold and diamonds. They were so pretty. She moved forward, toward the dress.

Suddenly, Bubbles felt someone grab her by one of her blond pigtails.

"What do you think you're doing, Bubbles?" Buttercup hissed. "Stay away from Princess. You know she's bad news."

"Don't you remember the way she tried to buy superpowers for herself so she could force her way into The Powerpuff Girls?" Blossom reminded her.

"Oh, right," Bubbles said. She felt bad. She knew that Princess was supposed to be The Powerpuff Girls' enemy.

But still, it was a beautiful dress.

The next day!

Bubbles was working at the glue table. She was pasting together a beautiful collage of sequins, sparkles, doilies, paper flowers, and velvet ribbons. The collage reminded her of Princess's dress.

"Hi, Bubbles," said a voice above her.

Bubbles looked up. It was Princess. She wasn't wearing the special dress today. But she was wearing a brand-new sparkling crown on her head.

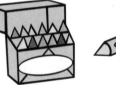

Bubbles's eyes grew wider as she looked at the crown. "That's so pretty!"

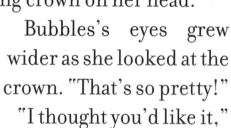

"I thought you'd like it," Princess said with a smug smile. "It's real diamonds, you know. And just look at THESE." She put a foot up on the glue table. "My shoes squirt Crystal Dawn Rose Petal Mist perfume when I walk," Princess said.

"Really?" Bubbles tried to imagine what it would feel like to walk around in a pretty-smelling cloud.

"That's right," Princess said. "Crystal Dawn Rose Petal Mist is my SIGNATURE scent. My daddy had it created especially for ME. Hey, wanna see my new jewel-covered scratch 'n' sniff stickers?"

"Those are the prettiest stickers ever!" Bubbles gasped.

Princess tossed the sheet on the table. "You can use some for your picture if you want," she said. "I've got MILLIONS."

"Oh, boy! Thanks so much!" Bubbles squealed. *Wow,* she thought, *this is going to be my most prettiest collage ever!*

Just then Blossom and Buttercup zoomed over to the table.

"All right, Princess, leave our sister alone," Buttercup said threateningly.

"Yeah," Blossom added. "I think it's about time for you to find another constructive activity at a different table."

Princess sneered. "You think you can push everyone else around just because you're superheroes. Well, I can stay right here with Bubbles if I feel like it, and you CAN'T make me leave!"

"We can if you're bothering our sister!" Buttercup threatened.

"Oh, Princess isn't bothering me," Bubbles piped up.

"She's not?" Blossom looked surprised.

Bubbles shook her head. "No, she's sharing really nicely. See? She gave me these stickers to put on my picture."

"Yeah, see?" Princess sneered again. "Now BUZZ OFF, Pesty-puffs! Me and my friend Bubbles are gonna make some more pretty pictures now."

Blossom and Buttercup stared at Bubbles.

"That's right," Princess went on, smirking. "And then after school, my

PAL Bubbles is gonna come over and play with my baby animal petting zoo."

"Princess! What are you saying?" Bubbles cried.

"You tell her, Bubbles," Blossom said. "Go ahead. Tell her there's no way you'll ever be friends with someone like her!"

Bubbles was staring at Princess. "What do

you mean? Do you really have a baby animal petting zoo?"

"Sure," Princess said. "Puppies, kittens, ducklings, bunnies — the works."

"Wow," Bubbles sighed. She loved baby animals.

"Bubbles, you can't go!" Buttercup yelled. "Princess is our enemy!"

But Bubbles wasn't so sure. After all, Princess had given her those pretty stickers. She was starting to seem like a pretty nice person after all. Besides, Bubbles was getting a little tired of the way her sisters were always bossing her around.

Bubbles was determined to make up her own mind. *After all*, she thought, *can't I be friends with anybody I want?*

Well, yes, I suppose so, Bubbles. But does it have to be Princess?

Chapter 2

The biggest house in Townsville! The sprawlingest, sparkliest, gaudiest, goldenest mansion of them all! Morbucks Manor!

Bubbles patted a baby bunny on the head. She and Princess were sitting in a pile of hay at Princess's petting zoo.

"You're so lucky to have all these baby animals, Princess," Bubbles said.

"I know," Princess said, absentmindedly twirling a puppy's ear. "Come on,

I'm SICK of this. Let's go look at my toys and find something else to do."

She led Bubbles down a carpeted, chandeliered hallway and stopped in front of an enormous golden door. Princess took a huge key ring out of her pocket.

"Let's see," she said, going through the keys one by one. "Tennis courts, swimming pool, bowling alley —"

"Wow!" Bubbles sighed. "You have all that stuff?"

"Sure," Princess replied. "Video arcade, paint-ball arena, toy room number one, toy room number two, toy room number thr —"

"You keep your toys locked up?" Bubbles was surprised.

"Of COURSE," Princess said. "Daddy and I keep EVERYTHING locked up."

"We don't keep anything locked up," Bubbles said, thinking. "The Professor doesn't even lock his lab!"

"Really," said Princess. "That's VERY interesting." She found the key she was looking for and opened the huge door. Inside was an enormous room filled with toys.

"Wow," Bubbles said, looking at all the stuff. She spotted a particularly beautiful doll. It had long, sparkling golden curls, and it was wearing a dress of silver and gold with pink lace ruffles. "That's the prettiest doll I've ever seen."

Princess picked up the doll. "Oh, that's my Lovely Lucy doll," she said. She handed it to Bubbles. Princess looked at Bubbles slyly. "You can have it, Bubbles."

Bubbles's eyes filled with tears of happiness. "I can? Really?"

"Yeah, I'm pretty sure I have another one in here just like it, only newer," Princess said. She began toss-  ing toys from the shelves. "Where IS that thing?" Finally, she pulled out a brand-new doll, still in its box. "There," she said, ripping open the box. "Now we have MATCHING Lovely Lucy dolls. Now they can be FRIENDS, just like us. RIGHT, Bubbles? Come on, let's take our Lovely Lucy dolls swimming in one of my pools."

As the girls changed into their bathing suits, Bubbles thought about Professor Utonium. "I guess the Professor buys us pretty nice stuff, too," she said. "But mostly it's stuff we need, like toothpaste and books and tights."

"But YOUR daddy gave you the best present ever," Princess said as they headed toward the pool. "Superpowers."

"Oh, yeah," Bubbles said, giggling.

"So, um, how'd he do that, anyway?" Princess asked, looking at Bubbles.

"Chemical X," Bubbles explained. "You see, when he was mixing together all the ingredients for the perfect little girls, some Chemical X accidentally got put in. And that's why me and Blossom and Buttercup are superheroes."

"Chemical X, huh? I'll tell Daddy to get

me some. I'd make a really GREAT super-hero, you know," Princess said.

Bubbles giggled. "Oh, I don't think you can buy Chemical X. I mean, the Professor has plenty in his lab. But I think you probably have to be a science person or something like that to get it."

When she heard this, Princess gritted her teeth angrily. Her face began to get red. She stomped her feet, and smoke puffed out of her ears.

"Princess, are you okay?" Bubbles asked with concern.

Princess made some strangled-sounding noises. Finally, she managed to take some deep breaths. Slowly, her feet stopped stomping and the redness drained from her face.

Bubbles was really worried about her friend. "Are you all right?"

"Fine," Princess replied with determination. "It was just a little . . . uh, fit, that's all. It happens sometimes when I — never mind. I'm FINE. Come on, let's go in the pool."

"Blossom has fits like that sometimes, too," Bubbles assured her friend as they swam. "It happens whenever she hears fingernails on a chalkboard."

"Oh, yeah?" Princess asked.

Bubbles giggled. "It's funny, because Blossom's such a great superhero. But just one scratch on a chalkboard can make her crumble!"

Princess looked at Bubbles intently. "Oh, REALLY?"

Bubbles giggled. "Don't tell her I told you, though. She probably wants to keep it a secret."

"I'll NEVER tell," Princess promised.

After a little while, Princess and Bubbles decided to get out of the pool and take their dolls to Princess's skating rink. As Bubbles zoomed around the huge ice rink with her Lovely Lucy doll, she felt like she had never been happier. Princess was such a good friend!

When the girls got off the ice, Princess handed Bubbles a green towel to wipe off the blades of her skates.

"Oh, this looks just like Buttercup's blankie!" Bubbles exclaimed, holding up the towel.

"Buttercup's WHAT?" Princess stared at her.

Bubbles giggled. "I know it sounds funny, 'cause Buttercup is so supertough. But she has this special blanket that she keeps in our room."

"She DOES?" Princess asked.

Bubbles nodded. "Don't tell her I told you, though. She'd probably be mad."

"I would never tell," Princess promised. She raised her hand. "BEST friend's honor."

"Best friend?" Bubbles repeated. Her heart felt full of happiness.

Best friend? Oh, no! Say it isn't so! Bubbles, Princess isn't your best friend, is she?

Chapter 3

The next evening at The Powerpuff Girls' house!

Bubbles, Blossom, and Buttercup were sitting at the table, eating dinner. Bubbles was telling her sisters all about Princess's house.

"And she has a riding ring with ponies in it, and a bobsled course, and a carousel . . ." Bubbles was explaining.

"Zip it, Bubbles," Buttercup snarled. "We don't want to hear it, okay?"

Just then, the hotline rang. Blossom zipped over to the phone. "Yes? What's that, Mayor? No problem, we'll be right there!" She turned to her sisters. "Mojo Jojo is destroying downtown Townsville!"

The Girls knew this was an emergency indeed. Mojo Jojo was an evil supergenius monkey. Townsville was in big trouble.

The Girls zoomed off to fight Mojo. They found him smack in the middle of downtown Townsville, by the Townsville Bank. Mojo was flying around the bank in his Mojo-Roto, blasting away the walls. Piles of money were falling onto the street.

"Mojo, you stop that right now!" Blossom warned.

"Bwa-ha-ha! You cannot stop me this time, Powerpuff Girls!" Mojo roared. He continued blasting the bank.

"Come on, Girls, let's get him," Blossom directed. She zipped up to the top of the Mojo-Roto and grabbed one of the whirring blades. The copter began to sputter.

Bubbles zoomed up beside Blossom. She began to shake the copter.

"Stop that this instant! Do not do that anymore!" Mojo yelled.

"Get ready, Buttercup," Blossom called. "Here he comes!"

Mojo tumbled out of the copter and landed on the ground. Buttercup headed straight for him. "Watch out, Mojo!" she yelled.

"Bwa-ha-ha! You are no match for me,

Powerpuff Girl Butter-
cup!" Mojo yelled at her.
"You are no match for
anyone! You are
merely a baby who
misses her blankie!"

Buttercup froze. "What
did you say?"

"I said you are just a little baby
who left her blankie at home in her
room!" Mojo taunted. "You are no match
for anyone."

Buttercup was so stunned she couldn't
move. With a final evil laugh, Mojo stood
up and dashed away.

Blossom and Bubbles let go of the
Mojo-Roto. They flew over to check on
their sister.

Just then a long, shiny, silver limousine

pulled up at the corner. The door opened and Princess hopped out.

"Hi, Powerpuff Girls," she said. "Looks like you guys could use a little HELP. Want me to pitch in? I'd be a GREAT superhero, you know."

"No way!" Blossom yelled at her.

"Maybe it's not such a bad idea," Bubbles said.

"It's a terrible idea," Blossom snapped back at her. "Get out of here, Princess!"

"Well, I was only trying to HELP!" Princess said huffily. She climbed back into her limousine and drove off.

Buttercup was still stunned. "How did he know?" she asked, her voice almost a whisper. "How could Mojo Jojo have known about my blankie?"

"It doesn't make any sense," Blossom said. "It's supposed to be a secret."

"Yeah," Bubbles echoed softly.

The next morning!

Bubbles, Blossom, and Buttercup were sitting at the table, eating the breakfast that the Professor had made them. Bubbles was feeding her Lovely Lucy doll.

Just then, the hotline rang.

Blossom zoomed over to the phone and picked it up. "Yes? What's that, Mayor? No problem, we'll be right there!" She turned to her sisters. "The Gangreen Gang is destroying the Townsville Mall!"

The Gangreen Gang was a grungy group of horrible hoodlums. Townsville was in trouble again. The Girls immediately flew off to confront them.

They found Ace, Little Arturo, Big Billy, Snake, and Grubber at the Townsville Mall, by the Townsville Treats Ice-Cream Shoppe. Ace was throwing benches through the shop's window. Big Billy and Snake were tipping over vats of ice cream. Grubber was eating spoonfuls of chocolate sauce, and Little Arturo was spitting into the nuts.

"Gangreen Gang, you stop that right now!" Blossom warned.

"Forget it, Powerpuff Girls!" Ace replied. He threw another bench.

"Come on, Girls, let's get them," Blossom directed.

Buttercup zoomed over to Billy and Snake. She lifted a vat of Pralines and Cream in one hand and a vat of

Chocolate Fudge Brownie in the other. "Take that!" she yelled, hurling the vats on top of Billy and Snake.

Bubbles flew over to Little Arturo. "It's not nice to spit in your food!" She picked him up and tossed him out the window.

Blossom was busy tying up Grubber with licorice strings. When she finished, she turned to the leader of the gang. "Okay, Ace, it's your turn now!"

"Oh, yeah?" Ace laughed an evil laugh. He reached into his pocket and pulled out a piece of chalkboard. He started to scratch on it with his fingernails.

"Aaaah!" Blossom yelled. "Aaahhh! Stop! Stop!" Blossom collapsed in a writhing heap on the floor of the mall.

"Come on, guys!" Ace called, quickly untying Grubber. "Let's get out of here!"

The gang escaped. Buttercup and Bubbles zoomed over to Blossom.

"Are you okay, Blossom?" Bubbles asked.

Just then a long, shiny, silver limousine pulled up, right into the mall. The door opened and Princess hopped out.

"Hi, Powerpuff Girls," she said. "Sure you guys don't want a little HELP?"

"Get lost!" Buttercup yelled at her.

"Um, thanks anyway," Bubbles said, trying to be nice.

"Suit yourself," Princess said huffily. "You'll change your mind eventually." She climbed back into her limousine and drove off.

Blossom was still stunned. "How could Ace have known about my blackboard weakness?"

Buttercup shook her head. "It's supposed to be a family secret."

"Yeah," Bubbles echoed softly.

"Just like you and your blanket," Blossom said thoughtfully.

"Nobody knows this stuff about us except us!" Buttercup said.

"And the Professor," said Blossom.

"And Princess," Bubbles added.

"What?!" Blossom and Buttercup yelled together.

"Well, I did mention something to Princess," Bubbles said. "But I'm sure she wouldn't tell anybody."

"What are you talking about?" Blossom said. "Of course she would tell!"

"She's our enemy, you ninny!" Buttercup cried.

Bubbles folded her arms across her chest. "She may be your enemy. But she's my friend. In fact, she's my best friend."

Oh, no, Bubbles! Can't you see? With a friend like Princess, you don't need enemies!

Chapter 4

Later that day!

The Powerpuff Girls flew home, exhausted from all their fighting. They flopped down on the living room couch.

"I can't believe we lost two fights in one day," Buttercup grumbled. She looked at Bubbles. "And it's all her fault!"

"No it isn't!" Bubbles objected.

"Girls, I have a plan," Blossom announced. "I think I know how we can round up Mojo, the Gangreen Gang, and any other criminals who think they can get the better of The Powerpuff Girls."

Buttercup perked up. "Oh, yeah? How?"

"Okay, we'll pretend to leave Townsville and go on a weekend trip," Blossom explained. "We'll make sure everyone in Townsville knows we're leaving. Then when all the criminals think it's safe to come out and make trouble, we'll surprise them with an attack."

Bubbles giggled. "Oooo, that's sneaky."

Buttercup shot her a look. "Yeah, and remember, Bubbles, it's also a secret!"

"Buttercup is right, Bubbles," Blossom said sternly. "You can't tell anyone about this."

"Okay, don't worry, I won't," Bubbles promised. "My lips are sealed!"

The next day! On the playground at Pokey Oaks — uh-oh! Bubbles, is that Princess you're talking to?

Bubbles was on the swings. Princess was sitting on the swing next to hers.

"Hey, Bubbles," Princess said. "Do you want to bring your Lovely Lucy doll over to MY house to play in my NEW life-sized Crystal Rainbow Cinderella Palace?"

Bubbles thought a moment. *I can go over to Princess's house*, she told herself. *I never promised I wouldn't do that. I can play with Princess without telling her the secret plan.*

Oh, no! Bubbles, don't do it! It's a mistake!

Later that day, Bubbles and Princess sat next to the Crystal Rainbow Cinderella Palace with their dolls.

"I can't BELIEVE your sisters wouldn't let me help fight," Princess complained. "I would make a great superhero, Bubbles. YOU know that." She sighed. "All I'd need is the superpowers."

Bubbles nodded. *Princess probably would be a pretty good superhero if she had powers*, Bubbles thought. It wasn't fair that some people were created with superpowers and some weren't.

Princess leaned forward. "Wanna hear a

secret, Bubbles?" she whispered. "I think I might be getting some superpowers after all, REAL soon. Wouldn't that be GREAT? Then we could both be super-heroes TOGETHER!"

"That would be so much fun," Bubbles agreed. She imagined herself fighting bad guys alongside Princess and then making pretty hairdos on their Lovely Lucy dolls together.

"But you can't tell ANYONE," Princess warned her. "It's a big SECRET."

"Don't worry, Princess," Bubbles said. "I won't tell anyone at all."

Princess narrowed her eyes. "How can I be sure?" she demanded.

"I really won't, Princess," Bubbles insisted. "I promise. Best friend's honor!"

"I know!" Princess said. "You tell me a

secret, too. That way we can each be sure the other won't tell."

Bubbles hesitated. She had a pretty big secret, but her sisters had told her not to tell it to anyone. Still, Princess had told Bubbles her secret.

"Best friends don't keep secrets from each other," Princess said.

"Okay," Bubbles said. "I'll tell you. But you have to promise not to tell anyone."

Princess raised her hand with a smile. "Best friend's honor."

Chapter 5

The next day! Oh, my, look at that. The Powerpuff Girls seem to be, ahem, ahem, leaving on a little trip. And it looks like all of Townsville has gathered to see them off.

Blossom, Bubbles, and Buttercup stood outside with their luggage. A huge crowd had gathered outside their house. A giant banner that said BON VOYAGE was strung across the street. The Mayor stood on a podium, waving. A band played.

Blossom looked around as the Professor loaded their suitcases into the car.

"Well, here we go," Blossom said. "Off on our trip!"

"That's right!" Buttercup agreed. "Bye, everyone!"

"I sure hope Townsville will be safe without us!" Blossom said loudly. "I sure hope no criminals try anything!"

The Girls all piled in the car with the Professor.

"Good-bye, Girls! Have a good trip!" the Mayor called out with a wink.

Bubbles sniffed as they drove away. "I sure am going to miss Townsville."

"Bubbles, we're not really leaving, remember?" Blossom said. "It's all part of my plan."

"Yeah," Buttercup snickered. "What

we're really going to do is kick some bad-guy butt!"

As soon as they were out of sight of the crowd, Blossom turned to the Professor. "Okay, pull around back."

With a screech, the Professor turned a sharp left. He drove around to the back door of the house. The Girls got out and sneaked back inside.

Blossom smiled. "Now all we have to do is wait for the criminals to come out."

And wait.

And wait.

And wait.

Two days later, they were still waiting.

"What's up with the criminals?" Butter-cup complained for the forty-third time.

"Maybe they all decided to go on trips, too," Bubbles suggested.

"No way," Blossom replied. "The statistical chances of every criminal in Townsville going away for the exact same weekend are . . . exactly one in six thousand nine hundred and fifty-six."

"We could always make more cocoa and watch another TV Puppet Pals video," Bubbles suggested.

"I'm tired of those dumb Puppet Pals videos," Buttercup complained. "I want to beat up some bad guys!"

Finally, the hotline rang. Blossom jumped up.

"This could be it, Girls!" She flew over to the phone. "Hello? Mayor? Hold on. I'm going to put you on speakerphone."

"Well, Girls, your plan worked," the Mayor's voice said. "This has been the quietest, most crime-free two-day period in Townsville history! Congratulations!"

"But Mayor, that wasn't the point!" Blossom said. "We wanted the criminals to come out this weekend."

"Yeah, so we could beat 'em up!" Buttercup added.

"Oh, well, a minor detail. I just wanted to let you Girls know what a good job you're doing. Bye!" The Mayor hung up.

Blossom flew back to her sisters, dejected. "My plan was a failure!" she said. "I don't understand it!"

"It's like the criminals knew what we were doing!" Buttercup complained.

"Bubbles, did you tell anyone?" Blossom demanded.

"No!" Bubbles insisted.
"No! Well, not any crim-
inals, at least."

"Bubbles!" Buttercup
wailed.

"You told Princess, didn't
you?!" Blossom accused.

"Well, she's my friend," Bubbles said.
"Best friends don't keep secrets from each
other. Besides, I'm sure Princess didn't tell
anyone else. She promised she wouldn't."

The hotline rang again. Blossom picked it
up. "Hello? Who?! What?!"

She turned to Bub-
bles with a scowl.
"Bubbles, it's Princess!
How did she get our
hotline number?"

"Well, it's my hotline,

too, isn't it?" Bubbles said hotly. "So I can give the number out to anyone I want." She flew over and took the phone. "Hi, Princess."

"Hi, Bubbles," Princess said. "I'm calling to invite you for a sleepover."

"Why sure, I'd love to come for a sleepover," Bubbles said. "I'll be right over." She hung up.

"Bubbles, you're not going!" Blossom said.

"No way!" Buttercup agreed.

"You guys can't boss me around," Bubbles said. "You're always trying to tell me what to do. Well, this time, I'm deciding for myself. And I decided that I like Princess and I think she's really nice and she shares all her pretty stuff with me and that's that!"

chapter 6

Later that night, Bubbles and Princess got ready to climb into Princess's queen-sized pink satin canopy bed. The two girls were wearing matching lavender velvet pajamas with white feather trim. Their Lovely Lucy dolls were wearing the exact same style of pajamas.

Right before she climbed into bed, Bubbles reached into her overnight bag. She pulled out Octi, her stuffed octopus.

Princess stared at her in surprise. "What's THAT thing?"

Bubbles smiled. "This is Octi. I sleep with him every single night. Octi, meet Princess. Princess, meet Octi." Bubbles made one of Octi's tentacles wave at Princess.

"But Bubbles, don't you want to sleep with your Lovely Lucy doll?" Princess asked. "I'm gonna sleep with mine."

"Oh, no thanks. I always sleep with Octi," Bubbles explained. "I've had him ever since . . ." Bubbles thought. She couldn't remember a time when she hadn't had Octi. "Since as long as I can remember, I guess. He's been around for ages!"

"He looks it, too," Princess muttered.

Bubbles stared at her friend, hurt. Then she shook her head. Princess was probably just making a joke.

The next day at Pokey Oaks Kindergarten!

Ms. Keane stood in front of the class. It was Sharing Time.

"Who has some news to share?" Ms. Keane asked the children.

Elmer Sglue raised his hand. "I do. I ate paste today."

Ms. Keane sighed. "Elmer, you're supposed to try to share something new. You can't keep sharing the same news every day. Okay, thanks anyway."

Princess raised her hand.

"Yes, Princess," Ms. Keane said. "What would you like to share with us?"

Bubbles turned to look at her new friend eagerly. She wondered what exciting new thing Princess was going to tell them about. Maybe Princess had a new pet elephant. Then Bubbles remembered the secret Princess had told her — about how she was going to have superpowers soon. Maybe Princess was going to share that!

Princess stood up. "I'd like to share something that I just learned," she said.

"Oh, good," Ms. Keane responded with a big smile. "We all want to be lifelong learners in this class, children."

Princess looked around at the group of children. "What I learned is that Bubbles sleeps with a dirty old stuffed octopus every night!" she announced.

The other kids burst out laughing.

"All right, children, that's enough! That's enough!" Ms. Keane said.

Bubbles felt tears stinging her eyes. How could Princess do this to her?

Chapter 7

Later that night! Oh, no, Bubbles! Are you crying?

Bubbles lay on her bed and hugged Octi. Her tears slid down her face and onto Octi's worn fabric. She heard her sisters turn on the television downstairs. She knew they were getting ready to watch the TV Puppet Pals. That was Bubbles's favorite show. But tonight she didn't feel like watching. Bubbles kept hearing Princess's words echo in her head. "Bubbles sleeps with a dirty old stuffed octopus every night!"

Bubbles held up Octi and looked at him. He was patchy and bald in places. And the stuffing was coming out of a seam on one tentacle.

"Oh, Octi, I guess you are worn and old. I never noticed before. And even when you were new, you were never fancy like a Lovely Lucy doll. I guess nobody would ever call you beautiful," Bubbles said softly. "Nobody but me!"

Suddenly, Bubbles was mad — really mad. She felt like a volcano was about to explode inside her. How dare Princess insult her Octi? Octi meant more to Bubbles than a thousand Lovely Lucy dolls.

Suddenly, there was a scream from downstairs. It was the Professor.

Bubbles dropped Octi and zoomed out into the hall. The Professor was standing on the

stairs. Blossom and Buttercup flew in from the living room.

"What's the matter?" Blossom asked.

"Are you okay?" Bubbles said.

The Professor's face had gone completely white. "Someone's been in my lab! A thief!" he cried. "There's only one thing missing — Chemical X!"

"Oh, no!" Bubbles gasped. So that's

where Princess planned to get her super-powers! Well, not if Bubbles could help it.

"But who would do something like that?" Blossom asked.

"I know who!" Bubbles announced. "Come on, Girls. Follow me."

"Where are we going?" Blossom wanted to know.

Bubbles scowled. "Morbucks Manor."

"We're right behind you!" Buttercup replied.

At Morbucks Manor, the Girls burst in to find Princess in a huge pink-marble bathtub filled with Crystal Dawn Rose Petal Mist-scented bubbles.

"Hey!" Princess yelled. "What are you doing here? I didn't invite YOU over!"

"Looks like we invited ourselves, Princess," Bubbles snarled.

"Oh, yeah?" Princess reached for a pink sequined bathrobe with a long silver cape. "Well, you got here just in time. I was just about to serve myself a refreshing drink — of CHEMICAL X!"

Princess reached for a large white container labeled CHEMICAL X.

Blossom gasped. "You stole that from the Professor!"

Princess smiled. "That's right. The door was unlocked just like Bubbles told me. It was easy. And now I'm going to take a great big gulp of it." She laughed. "If just a few drops of this stuff made YOU three into superheroes, imagine what a whole GALLON can do for ME!"

"Let's get her, Girls!" Bubbles called.

She snatched the Chemical X away from Princess. Buttercup zoomed over and knocked Princess into the bathtub.

Blossom zipped in and picked Princess up out of the water. She grabbed Princess by her silver cape and swung her around. Finally, Blossom let go, sending Princess flying. She crashed into a tower of perfume bottles. Then she stood up and raced out of the room.

"After her!" Bubbles cried.

The Girls followed Princess down the hall and into the toy room. When she came out, she had a fancy-looking laser shooter in her hand.

Princess grinned an evil grin. "I've got you now, Powerpuff Girls," she said, waving the laser. "This thing can destroy all three of you at once!"

"Watch out, Girls!" Blossom warned.

But Bubbles took off straight toward the laser. She focused her eye beams on it.

"Bubbles, be careful!" Buttercup yelled.

Bubbles kept her eye beams on the laser. It began to smoke. Finally, it dissolved into a pile of melted plastic in Princess's hands.

"Nothing but an expensive toy!" Bubbles scoffed. "Just like everything you own, Princess. You'll never be the real thing!"

"She's getting away!" Blossom yelled as Princess darted behind her life-sized Crystal Rainbow Cinderella Palace to hide.

Bubbles looked around. She spotted Princess's Lovely Lucy doll nearby. She

scooped it up. Using the doll as a club, Bubbles began to smash away at the palace's walls.

"My NEW life-sized Crystal Rainbow Cinderella Palace! It's ruined! I wasn't even sick of it yet!" Princess wailed.

Blossom flew in and grabbed Princess by her robe. She tossed her to Buttercup, who threw her straight into a pen in the petting zoo. Bubbles zoomed over and locked the door to the pen.

"Yuck! These aren't cute little lambs anymore!" Princess complained from inside the pen. "They're big, smelly sheep!"

Bubbles giggled. "Say hello to your new signature scent, Princess!"

"Well, that ought to hold her until the police get here," Blossom said. "I guess our job is done, Girls."

"Not quite," Bubbles said. She looked

down at the Lovely Lucy doll in her hands. Suddenly, it didn't seem lovely at all. With a quick twist she pulled off its head. "Here, Princess," she said, tossing it into Princess's pen. "This is from Octi!"

Bubbles turned to her sisters. "I can't believe Princess actually thought she had what it takes to be a Powerpuff Girl. And I can't believe I fell for it! I'm sorry. I promise never to confuse sparkles and rainbows with friendship ever again."

And so, once again, the day was saved, thanks to The Powerpuff Girls!